I'll See You
When the Moon Is Full

by SUSI GREGG FOWLER   pictures by JIM FOWLER

SILVER BURDETT GINN

Library of Congress Cataloging-in-Publication Data
Fowler, Susi Gregg
I'll see you when the moon is full / by Susi Gregg Fowler;
illustrations by Jim Fowler.
        p.   cm.
Summary: Abe will miss his father when he takes off on
a business trip but is reassured of his return
in two weeks, when the crescent moon becomes full.
ISBN 0-688-10830-X (trade). ISBN 0-688-10831-8 (lib.)
[1. Fathers and sons — Fiction.
2. Separation anxiety — Fiction.
3. Moon — Fiction.]   I. Fowler, Jim, ill.   II. Title.
PZ7.F82975Il   1994   [E] — dc20
91-47667   CIP   AC
      97 98 99 00 -MZ- 6 5 4 3   ISBN   0-382-33644-5

In memory of Grandpa, Jim Gregg,
who gave me the moon
—S. G. F.

For Quentin Fowler
—J. F.

"**W**ill you miss me?" Abe asked. He handed Daddy a stack of folded shirts.

"I always miss you when I'm gone," Daddy said, packing the shirts in his suitcase.

"How much?" Abe asked.

Daddy stopped packing and scratched the top of his head. "I miss you so much that my hair falls out," he said.

Abe giggled.

"And I miss you so much that sometimes I forget to take notes in my meetings. I draw pictures of you and me fishing, instead."

"You do?" said Abe.

Daddy nodded. "And I miss you so much that sometimes I feel like crying when I know I have to go on another trip."

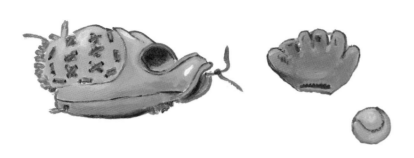

"I miss you when you're gone," said Abe.
"How much?" asked Daddy.

Abe scratched his head. "I miss you so much that I can't go to bed on time," he said.

"I heard about that," said Daddy.

"And I miss you so much that I draw pictures all day long of you and me doing things."

"Will you save me some of those?" asked Daddy.

Abe nodded and said, "I miss you so much that sometimes the only things that will make me feel better are ice cream and extra stories."

"Your mother mentioned that," said Daddy.

Abe sighed. "I wish you didn't have to go now," he said.

"I know," said Daddy. "But I'll be back."

"When?" asked Abe.

"In two weeks," said Daddy.

"How long is that?" asked Abe.

His father thought a minute. "It will be when the moon is full," he answered.

"When will that be?" asked Abe.

"Come look out the window," said his father.

    A tiny sliver of white shone in the night sky where just the night
before there had been no sign of the moon.

"Do you remember how the moon changes?" asked Daddy.

"Tell me," said Abe.

"What we see now is just part of the moon. We call it a crescent
moon," said Daddy.

"Crescent moon?" Abe repeated.

"Yes," said Daddy. "But the moon doesn't always look this way, does it?"

Abe shook his head. "Sometimes it's bigger," he said.

"That's right," said Daddy. "It seems to grow because we see a little more of it each night. In about a week we'll see a half moon, and then it will keep getting bigger and bigger, night after night, until finally..." He paused and looked at Abe. "You tell me."

"Until the moon is full!" Abe shouted.

"That's it," said Daddy.

"And then it will get skinny again, right?" said Abe.

"Yes," said Daddy. "But before it starts getting smaller again, I'll be home."

"I have an idea," said Abe. "I'll draw a picture of the moon every night. Then I'll show you how the moon changed when you were gone."

"That's a great idea," said Daddy. "But some nights there might be clouds, so you won't see the moon."

"Then I'll just draw the clouds," Abe said.

"Good thinking," Daddy said. "And then the next night, or when the clouds are gone, the moon will be back, even bigger." He looked at Abe and smiled. "You can always count on the moon, and you can always count on me."

"Remember," said Daddy. "When you draw a moon that looks like a giant ball that's bounced up to the sky, I'll be home."

"That will be my favorite picture," said Abe.

"Mine, too," said Daddy. He snapped his suitcase closed.

Beep beep came a noise from outside.

Daddy checked his watch.

"There's my ride," he said.

He picked Abe up and squeezed him tightly. "I'm going to miss you!" he said.

Abe stood in the doorway, waving. "Good-bye, Daddy," he called.
"I'll see you when the moon is full!"
And like an echo Daddy answered, "I'll see you when the
moon is full!"